Daisy's Discovery

Story by Anne Kelley
Pictures by Metin Salih

BARRON'S

Woodbury, New York · London · Toronto · Sydney

For Almerinda and Hussein

It was going to be a bad day, thought Daisy. It had certainly begun badly. She had been having one of her favorite dreams—about food. There was a big box of chocolate cookies open in front of her. She was just about to take her first bite when there was an awful thump.

The chocolate cookies vanished. She woke up with a start. The puppy, Tom, had dropped a bone on her head.

Daisy snapped at Tom, but he didn't care. He·
didn't even say "sorry." He had no manners at all.
And he wouldn't let Daisy share his bone.
Watching Tom eat the bone made Daisy feel
hungry.

She trotted off into the garden. She remembered burying a juicy bone of her own out there last summer.

It had been somewhere behind the compost heap, she thought. She had fun digging, but the bone wasn't there.

Perhaps it hadn't been behind the compost heap
after all. She had quite forgotten where it was now.
She sat and scratched while she thought about it.
Then she remembered that she had seen a cookie
on Robert's bed, under his pillow.

"Well," she said to herself, "a little snack would
keep me going until lunch."

She searched and searched for the cookie. She was so busy looking that she didn't hear Mom come into Robert's bedroom.

Mom was cross. "You bad dog, Daisy. Whatever do you think you're doing?" she cried. "Look at your feet. And look at Robert's bed."

"I am looking at Robert's bed," thought Daisy. "And as far as I can see, there's nothing worth looking at." The cookie wasn't there, and Daisy was getting hungrier. Things weren't going right at all.

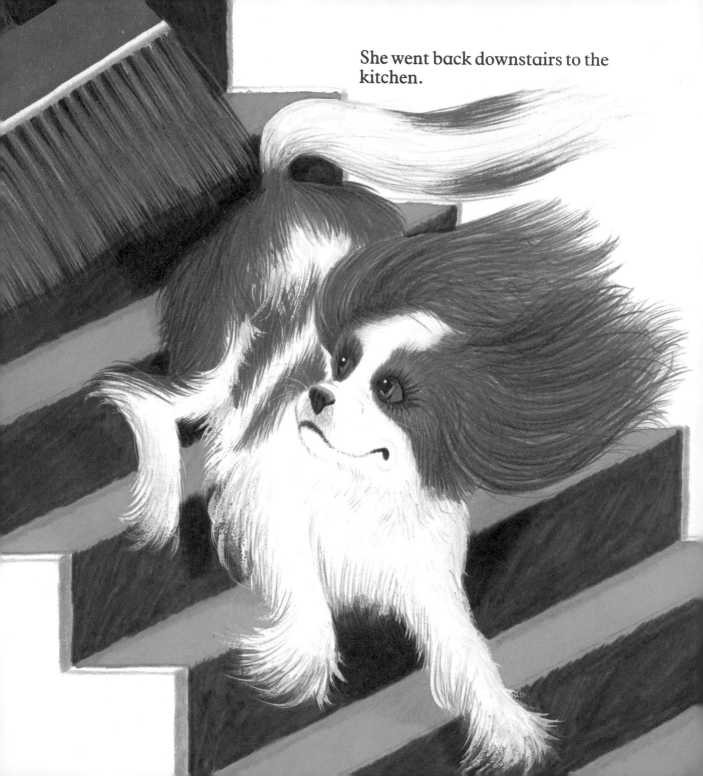

She went back downstairs to the kitchen.

Things weren't right in the kitchen, either. Mom and Dad were rushing about with bowls and saucepans. When Daisy tried to help, she was told to go and lie down in her basket.

Daisy thought she would go to see Robert and
Jane. They would give her something to eat. But
even Robert and Jane were too busy for Daisy
today.

   Robert was playing a new game with paper.
Daisy thought she would play, too, but Robert was
cross. "You're in the way, Daisy. Go to your
basket!" he cried.

Jane was blowing up balloons. They looked quite delicious. Daisy tried to eat one, but it went "bang!" and made Daisy jump. Jane was cross.

"Go away, Daisy, and don't be so silly. Go to your basket!" she cried.

"Everyone is cross today," thought Daisy as she lay in her basket. "Something dreadful must have happened."

She settled down to watch. There seemed to be more food than usual in the kitchen. It was a good idea to keep your eyes open, just in case some of the food dropped on the floor. Daisy knew it did that sometimes.

Suddenly Mom cried out, "My ring! I've lost my ring!"

"Are you sure?" asked Dad. The children came to look at Mom's bare finger.

"I had it this morning," replied Mom. She seemed very upset. "We'll have to look for it."

"But Mom, it's only two hours to my party, and we're not ready yet," said Jane, with tears in her eyes.

"I'll finish the food, sweetheart. You and Dad look for my ring," said Mom.

Dad and the children hunted everywhere for the ring. They looked under the table, in drawers, in cupboards, even in the dogs' basket. But there was no ring.

"Well, that's it," thought Daisy. "They've obviously forgotten all about our lunch. All that fuss about a ring. You can't even eat a ring."

She thought she might as well go
and have a walk around. You never
knew what you might find.

She went into the living room. And there, on a low table, was a wonderful surprise. Someone had left her a big, beautiful, pink and white cake. They had remembered her lunch after all!

She sniffed carefully round the cake, deciding where to start. Then she sank her teeth into it.

She had just eaten all she could, when she heard an awful howl.

"Daisy!" shrieked Jane. "Mom! Mom! Look what Daisy's done. She's eaten my birthday cake!" Jane began to cry.

Daisy looked round guiltily, her mouth full of
cake. There must have been a mistake. Perhaps
the cake hadn't been for her after all.

Mom and Dad appeared in the doorway. They
looked very, very cross.

Daisy tried to swallow her mouthful
quickly, but her teeth hit something
hard and scratchy. She yelped and
opened her mouth, and out fell . . .
A RING!

"Look, Mom! Look, Mom!" shouted Robert. "Daisy's found your ring! Isn't she clever!"

"It must have come off my finger when I was making the cake," said Mom, shaking her head in surprise.

So in the end, it wasn't such a bad day after all. Daisy was forgiven for eating the cake. She got a kiss from Mom, and a chocolate cookie.

She couldn't really manage to eat the cookie, so she let Tom have it instead.

Dad went to the bakery and bought Jane a new birthday cake.

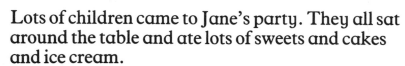

Lots of children came to Jane's party. They all sat around the table and ate lots of sweets and cakes and ice cream.

But who do you think was the guest of honor? That's right!

First U.S. edition published in 1985
by Barron's Educational Series, Inc.

© 1985 by Anne Kelley

This book has been designed and produced by Aurum Press Limited,
33 Museum Street, London WC1A 1LD.

All inquiries should be addressed to:
Barron's Educational Series, Inc.
113 Crossways Park Drive
Woodbury, New York 11797

International Standard Book No. 0–8120–5676–0

Library of Congress Catalog Card No. 85-9200

Printed in Belgium

5 4 3   9 8 7 6 5 4 3 2 1